Washday on Noah's Ark

A Story of Noah's Ark according to

GLEN ROUNDS

Holiday House / New York

Library of Congress Cataloging in Publication Data

Rounds, Glen, 1906–
Wash day on Noah's Ark.

Summary: When the forty-first day on the ark dawns
bright and clear, Mrs. Noah decides to do the wash,
and having no rope long enough, devises an ingenious
clothesline.

1. Children's stories, American. [1. Noah's ark—
Fiction. 2. Tall tales] I. Title.
PZ7.R761Was 1985   [E]   84-22380
ISBN 0-8234-0555-9
ISBN 0-8234-0880-9 (pbk.)

This is for my granddaughter,
MISS KATY,
with love and a vast appreciation
of her help in my learning to draw
left-handed

Many, many years ago a man named Noah listened to the weather reports predicting unusually heavy rains, and possible flooding. So he decided to build a boat big enough to hold his family and his farm animals—just in case.

All that summer he and his sons measured and sawed and hammered, building what they called an Ark. When they ran out of lumber, they tore down some old tobacco barns to get more.

On the top deck was a stout corral for the horses and cows, and downstairs they built pens to keep the pigs and smaller animals out of the family quarters. Noah was just painting THE ARK in big letters across the back when the first big drops of rain began to fall.

By the time the family had scurried onto the boat with their livestock and their pots, pans and bedding, the rain was coming down in sheets while great peals of thunder boomed from cloud to cloud.

Everything was loaded and Noah had just remarked that it looked like it was going to be a humdinger of a storm when a huge elephant came galloping up the swaying gangplank and disappeared inside!

And right behind the elephant came hundreds of other animals of every imaginable size and kind—pushing and shoving into every vacant space in the Ark.

Mrs. Noah was in a snit. She told Noah, "You've got to get those wild creatures out of here. An elephant is turning over my cook pots and monkeys are running off with the children's bedding. I'll not put up with it!"

"I'm not about to start messing around with all those lions,
tigers, rhinoceroses and other big critters in there," he an-
swered. "We'll just have to hope the rain stops by morning."

But the rain went on and on. And for forty days and forty nights the Ark floated here and there while Noah and his family stayed cooped up inside with all those roaring, squalling, barking, fighting, seasick animals.

"I wish the rain would stop!" Mrs. Noah said one day. "It's getting stuffy in here and a body can't hear herself think, what with the children and all these animals carrying on so!"

To keep the grandchildren out of mischief, Noah spent much
of his spare time telling them stories. And later he found
some sticks and old newspapers lying around and built them
a big kite.

Of course they couldn't fly it in all that rain and besides, they had no kite string. But the children were kept busy for days, with scissors and paste, decorating the kite with pictures cut from old magazines.

At last the rain *did* stop. When the Noahs looked out the window on the morning of the forty-first day, they saw that the sun was shining, and the Ark was floating quietly in the middle of a great sea of muddy water.

"Oh, what a beautiful washday!" Mrs. Noah exclaimed as she hurried to build a fire under the big washpot. For forty days and forty nights she'd been unable to do any laundry because of the rain, and now she had an enormous washing to do.

All morning Mrs. Noah and her daughters boiled, scrubbed,
rinsed and wrung out clothes. But when she asked Noah to
put up her clothesline, he said he'd forgotten to bring it.

When she asked him how she was going to dry all that wash without a clothesline, he agreed that it might be difficult, or even impossible, and went back to doctoring a sick camel.

But Mrs. Noah intended to dry her wash one way or another. So she stomped around the Ark, squeezing between the tightly packed animals, searching for something she could use for a clothesline.

Noticing what appeared to be a piece of stout cord hanging
from one edge of the big kite, she looked closer and found a
long green snake trying to hide between it and the wall. And
that gave her an idea.

She'd noticed that there were thousands of snakes hiding in
dark corners all over the Ark, so now she called to the grandchildren. "Go catch me some snakes," she told them. "Bring
me every one you can find."

It turned out to be the most fun the children had had in weeks—better than a scavenger hunt. They found brown snakes, yellow snakes and green snakes—spotted snakes and striped snakes—long snakes, short snakes and middle-sized snakes—snakes of all kinds.

And as fast as they carried the squirming creatures to Mrs.
Noah, she tied them together, head to tail, with firm square
knots, and coiled them neatly on the floor.

When she thought her string of snakes was long enough, she tied one end to the harness of the big kite. Holding firmly to the end of her strange kite string, she walked to the rail and tossed the kite into the air. It flopped and pinwheeled in the brisk wind at first, but soon she had it flying nicely.

Mrs. Noah braced herself against the pull of the kite while her daughters hung the wet clothes, piece by piece, on the strange clothesline and fastened them firmly with big wooden clothespins.

It was probably the strangest looking clothesline the world had seen up to that time. As the big kite sailed higher, the clothes flapped and snapped in the wind, already beginning to dry beautifully.

When all the clothes baskets were empty, Mrs. Noah tied the tail of the last snake to the rail with a clove hitch, then went downstairs to fix peanut butter sandwiches and tea for lunch.

After lunch Noah pulled the squirming line in while his wife unpinned and folded the clean clothes. And as he coiled the empty line on the deck, the children untied the knotted snakes and let them slither back to their hiding places.

KNUTE
THE LEFT HANDED

It had been a long and busy day for Mrs. Noah. But that night at supper, when she saw how nice her family looked after they'd all taken baths and put on clean clothes for the first time in forty days and forty nights, she figured that it had been well worthwhile.